Books for B

The Hunter

By

My books are a project to get my son to enjoy reading. The stories use early reading words and subject matter young boys like. The words in the book range from pre-primer through third grade words. Early readers will find reading and learning more enjoyable because of the appropriate and interesting content.

For all boys who find reading boring!

Making Reading Fun!

ISBN 978-1-304-01278-4

The Hunter

Fall is just around the corner and that means only one thing in our family. Hunting!

We start our day very early in the morning. I laugh at myself because I get up fast to go hunting but I get up slowly for school.

The birds are much better in early fall or so my dad tells me. I think my dad will let me carry the duck decoys to the water this year.

The first hunt is always so much fun for me. I make hot chocolate for my dad and myself. I get my gloves, hat, and old boots. I am ready to go.

I helped my dad clear out
some small trees last summer
to keep our duck blind clean.

"Good!" My dad is letting me carry the decoys; I better do a good job. "Oops!" My decoys feel light, I better count them. "One, two, three, four, five, six" I had seven when I started.

I better go back and look for my decoy. It has green and white colors with a short tail. I hope I did not drop it far away.

I found my decoy sitting in a bush. I pick up all the decoys and start for the blind with my dog.

I show up and my dad starts to laugh. He said, "You still have to grow up a little." I laughed at myself and said "Drink your hot chocolate. I will show you." He kept laughing.

I walk in the water when some big birds fly over my head. My dad says “Run fast!”

I start to walk to the duck blind; one step, two steps, three steps. My foot starts to feel cold as my boot fills fast with cold water.

I keep walking and try not to say anything to my dad. My feet are getting very cold now. I wish I had checked my boots last night for any holes like my dad told me to do.

He laughed and pulled another pair of boots out of a bag with dry socks and said, “Drink your hot chocolate!”

We both laughed together for a long time.

The End

Keep Reading!

More Books from Mr. 7 Yea!

My Rocket Ship

Cowboy

Fire Fighter

Runaway Sailboat

Cool Forts

The Fish that Ate Me

Lost Campers

Baseball Wars

Dinosaurs